THE FINTASTIC DIARY OF

Darcy Dolphin

First published in paperback in Great Britain 2017
by Egmont UK Limited
The Yellow Building, 1 Nicholas Road, London W11 4AN

Text copyright © 2017 Sam Watkins
Illustrations copyright © 2017 Vicky Barker
The moral rights of the author and illustrator have been asserted

ISBN 978 1 4052 8422 6

www.egmont.co.uk

65065/1

A CIP catalogue record for this title is available from the British Library

Printed and bound in Great Britain by the CPI Group

Stay safe online. Any website addresses listed in this book are
correct at the time of going to print. However, Egmont is not
responsible for content hosted by third parties.
Please be aware that online content can be subject to change and
websites can contain content that is unsuitable for children. We advise
that all children are supervised when using the internet.

MIX
Paper
FSC   FSC® C018306

CONTENTS

PHEE-WEEEEE!

(That means 'hello' in Dolphinese, in case whoever is reading this is not a dolphin.) Yesterday was my birthday and my aunt Ditzy gave me this book. She said it is a **diary**.

I've never had a diary so I didn't really know what to write in it. Aunt Ditzy wrote a recipe book called **Super Seaweed Smoothies**, so she is a proper real-life author. I don't think anyone has actually bought it yet, but anyway she knows loads about writing and books and stuff.

I asked her what you should write in a diary and she said, 'Oh, you know, feelings, that sort of thing.' I said I would try to write down at least one feeling a day.

So here goes – my first diary! Does that make me a proper author too, I wonder? I hope some interesting things happen this week. I can't write 'Went to school, had fish fingers for tea' every day, can I? That would make pretty boring reading. But I'm sure I'll have loads of exciting stuff to write about – I can just feel it in the water . . .

WEEK 1:
My Perfect Pet

MONKFISHDAY

So this morning I was feeling **excited**!

This is because in assembly Mr Snapper, the head teacher, announced that there is going to be a **pet show** on Salmonsday! There will be loads of different competitions for different skills, so if your pet is super-good at something you can enter them into that competition and maybe win a prize!

Our teacher, Miss Carp, stuck a big poster up on the classroom wall. Everyone crowded round to have a look. It was covered in stars and in big sparkly letters it said '**PETS FACTOR**'. Underneath that was a list of all the competitions. My friend Ozzie Octopus said that he will enter Cuke, his pet sea cucumber, in the 'Animal or Vegetable?' game. And Myrtle Turtle said she'd put Squishy, her vampire squid, in for the Talent Show. Squishy can turn herself completely inside out, which I think is quite talented.

I looked at the poster. 'Pet Fancy Dress – that sounds fun! I'm going to sign up for that one,' I said.

'But Darcy, you haven't *got* a pet,' Myrtle said.

'I'll ask Mum tonight if I can get one. She's bound to say yes.'

So earlier this evening I told Mum all about

the pet show and how I really wanted a pet.

Mum gave me her ☹ face and said, 'Darcy we've talked about this before and you know how I feel. Pets are too much trouble and blah blah blah blah blah . . . anyway, the answer is NO.'

I think she might be thinking about it.

Hmmph. Everyone has a pet except me. It's not fair.

New
↖ **Feeling of the Day:** ~~EXCITED~~ DEPRESSED.

Flippering fishsticks, I didn't realise you could have so many feelings in one day!

TUNASDAY

Last night I couldn't sleep thinking about how I could persuade Mum to let me have a pet. Then – **click**! I had a brainwave. Mum's always moaning she's got too much to do. If I was really, really helpful she might let me have a pet as a reward!

I got up **really** early so I could get as much helping done as possible. I even made a chart in case I needed proof of my helpfulness to show Mum (she can be *very* forgetful sometimes).

HELPFULNESS CHART

Morning:

5 am: Took Mum and Dad prawnflakes in bed. Dad groaned and Mum rolled over but I know they were secretly pleased.

5.30 am: Vacuumed the floor. Not a huge success. The vacfish got too full up and, well . . . it exploded!

6.30 am: Tidied the toy cave and got rid of loads of old toys. My little brother, Diddy, screamed his lungs out until I explained that it's for a good cause. Then he sulked in a corner all day refusing to eat.

7 am: Weeded the vegetable patch. I might have accidentally weeded some of Dad's prize sea lettuces, but I don't think he'll notice.

Afternoon:

4 pm: Helped Mum do the shopping. Mum never buys enough Jiggling Jellies, so I helped her by putting every bag on the shelf into the basket. Weirdly, Mum didn't seem to find that very helpful.

5 pm: Made dinner. I did fish fingers and mushy seaweed with Jiggling Jellies on top. Dad said he wasn't hungry, but I think he was impressed with my creative cookery skills.

6 pm: Washed up. Broke one or maybe several things. Well, we didn't need all those dishes, anyway. Dad's always moaning that there's too much washing up.

After dinner I said I would make Mum a nice cup of sea. She squeaked.

'NO! I mean, no thank you, Darcy.'

I was a bit hurt. 'But Mum . . . I thought if I was really helpful you might let me . . . um . . . have a pet?'

'A pet? I said yesterday –'

'Please? I'll be really good! I'll help all week!

I'll make dinner every day and I'll do the washing
. . . and the ironing . . . and . . .'

Mum's fins started twitching. 'OKAY!
Okay – you can get a pet. A *small* one. Just,
please, that's enough helping for today, Darcy!'

Dad looked as if he wanted to say something, but he had a mouthful of prawnflakes (weird – I thought he said he wasn't hungry?). But it didn't matter, because Mum said **yes**! Now I can't sleep again – thinking about all the adventures I'm going to have with my new pet!

Feeling of the Day: ECSTATIC.

WHALESDAY

Mum said she would take me to the pet shop
after school, so I spent all day trying to decide
what pet to get.

In Science, Miss Carp showed us a
video about human fry (you humans call
them 'children' I think). They're soooo cute!
Afterwards we had to fill in a factsheet about
what we'd learned. Here's mine . . .

HUMAN FRY – FACTSHEET

Diet:

Mainly ice cream and sand.

Appearance:

Have loads of very thin tentacles on their heads. Some have coloured rings of blubber around their bellies to help them float.

Habitat:

Beaches or boats.

Communication:

Make a lot of noise, but do not click or whistle like dolphins do. If a human fry drops an ice cream it makes a high-pitched squealing sound.

Then I had another brainwave – I could get
a **human** for a pet! I put my fin up. Miss
Carp looked at me. She likes us to ask good
questions.

'Yes, Darcy?'

'Would a human make a good pet?' I asked.

Everyone laughed. Miss Carp gave me
her '**I Am Not Amused**' look and said
that looking after a pet was a '**Serious
Matter**', and not to be '**Taken Lightly**'.

Hmmph – I am not taking it lightly! To prove
this, I went to the school library at lunchtime
and got a book called **THE PERFECT PET**.
It's all about pets and how to look after them.
There's nothing about humans in it though.

After school, Mum took me to Pollock's
Pet Shop. Mr Pollock was there, feeding the

17

sea horses. He smiled at me. 'So you're after a pet, eh? What sort were we thinking?'

'Something easy to look after, please,' Mum said, before I could speak.

'Easy, eh? Well, we've got some nice sea urchins.'

Mum was quite keen on the sea urchins until one spiked her on the nose.

'No, thank you,' she said.

'Do you have any humans?' I asked. For some reason Mr Pollock and Mum roared with laughter.

'How about a sea cucumber?' Mr Pollock said, fishing one out of a tank.

'Ooh – it could be friends with Cuke!' I said. As Mr Pollock handed it to Mum, it squirted a cloud of disgusting white goo all over her.

'**Eurrrgh**!' she said. 'Definitely not!'

When I picked up a starfish one of its legs fell off. Mr Pollock said that was normal. But I don't want a pet whose legs keep dropping off!

I can't believe it is this difficult to find a pet – and Pets Factor is only three days away! Where oh where can my perfect pet be?!

Feeling of the Day: FRUSTRATED.

TURTLESDAY

You'll never guess what happened today! We
had a school trip to the Kelp Forest, which is
a big forest of seaweed just the other side of
Ripple Reef. But that's not the exciting bit –
you'll have to wait for that!

When we arrived Miss Carp put us in
groups. I was with my friends Ozzie and
Myrtle, and also Angie Angelfish – worse luck!
Angie kept whingeing.

'The Kelp Forest is dangerous! My mum
says there are sharks there!'

'That's just an old fish's tale,' I said, looking round. The tall swaying kelp fronds blocked out most of the light, so it was really dark and gloomy. Miss Carp's voice made me jump.

'Okay pupils, you may go into the forest and collect your interesting specimens. Meet back here in half an hour. Stay with your groups and, whatever you do, DON'T go past the old treasure chest. That means EVERYONE . . .'

She gave me a **piercing** look when she said the last bit, I have no idea why.

Nervously we swam into the forest. We didn't see any sharks, thankfully. But we didn't find any interesting specimens either.

Then, just ahead, I saw the old treasure chest.

I peered over it into the gloom. Not far off, half buried in the sand, I thought I could see some interesting-looking specimens. With a flick of my tail I swam over the treasure chest and headed for them.

Angie started flipping out. 'Darcy! Miss Carp said . . .'

'Oh, come on. We won't go far . . . wow, look at this shiny pebble!'

'Ooh, let me see . . .' Angie swam over. She can't resist shiny things. Ozzie and Myrtle followed, reluctantly.

I spotted something else. 'Look! More interesting things!'

We swam a bit further.

'More over there!' Ozzie exclaimed, pointing.

'And here!' Myrtle shouted.

Soon we had a stack of **interesting specimens**:

- 37 pebbles (interestingly shaped)
- 4 shells (interestingly broken)
- 1 dead whelk (interestingly whiffy)

I put them all in the specimen bag. By then it was getting properly dark.

'Let's go and find the others,' Myrtle said.

We started swimming back. But everything looked different. The waving fronds of kelp looked bigger somehow. Big black rocks loomed all around us that I was sure we hadn't passed before. And the old treasure chest seemed to have vanished completely.

We were lost!

I actually got a little bit scared. Then Angie screamed really loudly in my ear.

'EEEEEEEEEEEEEEEEEK!!!'

'Flippering fishsticks, don't *do* that!' I gasped, but my eyes nearly popped out when I saw what she was squeaking about. A huge shadow was looming out from behind a clump of seaweed. Ozzie turned about fifteen different colours and Myrtle disappeared inside her shell so fast I thought she'd come out the other end. Angie darted behind me, babbling.

'A shark! A shark!'

The seaweed rustled and a teensy little fish swam out. I heaved a sigh of relief. Myrtle's head came back out of her shell and Ozzie's colour went back to normal.

We all laughed except Angie who stayed behind me, quivering.

'It's only a little fish, Angie!' said Ozzie.

'It might be a trick!' she whimpered.

Honestly, Angie is such a scaredy-sprat!

The fish looked at me and wagged its tail.

'You're cute,' I said. I swam one way, and the fish did too. I swam the other way, and so did the fish. I laughed.

'Go home, fishy,' I said. But the fish didn't move, it just kept staring at me, tail wagging madly. I started to swim away, but it followed me. 'It won't leave me alone!'

'Maybe it's hungry and can smell that dead whelk in your bag,' Ozzie said.

'I think it's a dogfish,' said Myrtle. 'It probably wants to play.'

'A dogfish...' I suddenly had a **tidal brainwave**. 'Dogfish make perfect pets –

it said so in that book I was reading. I think it wants to be my pet!'

I patted the dogfish on the head.

'It's okay, little fishy,' I said. 'You can be my pet.'

Feeling of the Day: CRAZY HAPPY!

FLOUNDERSDAY

PHEE-WEEEEE! I have a pet –
just in time for Pets Factor tomorrow! I've
named him Finley, because he's got a really
big dorsal fin.

It was a bit of a nightmare getting him
home yesterday – first I had to hide him in
the specimen bag so that when we *finally*
found the others, Miss Carp didn't confiscate
him. Then when we got back to school I opened
the specimen bag to find that he'd eaten all the
specimens – including the pebbles! Mum was

really difficult too. At first she said I should take him back to where I found him. But I begged and begged and I had to promise to do **everything** she told me without arguing for a whole MONTH before she finally said I could keep him.

'Well, I suppose dogfish do make good pets,' she said. 'But you'll have to house-train him, Darcy.'

I offered to make dinner again to say thank you, but I don't think she heard me.

When I got home from school today, I looked up house-training in the Perfect Pet book. It said:

'HOUSE TRAINING: You should make sure your pet has a special place to do its business.'

I was a bit confused by this, until Dad told me that 'business' is the grown-up word for 'poo'. Mum is doing potty-training with Diddy so I thought I could try it with Finley. Unfortunately, Finley would not stay on the potty, so I tied it to him. He hasn't done an actual business in it yet, but he keeps farting pebbles so I think it will happen soon.

The book had a useful list of things that you have to do for a pet. For example:

'FEEDING: Feed your pet healthy and nutritious food, once or twice a day. Do not over-feed your pet.'

I am trying not to overfeed Finley, but it's hard. He eats anything. Everything, in fact. He's eaten all the food in the house. He even tried to have a nibble on Diddy, but luckily Mum didn't see.

'SLEEPING. Give your pet somewhere cosy to sleep.'

I have made the toy cave into a home for Finley. The only problem is that he tries to bite anyone who goes in there.

'PLAY WITH YOUR PET. Pets enjoy a range of games and some may like having other pets to play with, too.'

Ozzie came round after school with Cuke and they had great fun playing chase. Finley chased Cuke mainly. Then Cuke went bright orange and starting squirting gooey stuff everywhere, and Ozzie said they had to go.

Before bed I got Finley's outfit ready for the fancy dress competition tomorrow. I'm going to put him in an old shark costume of Diddy's. He'll look so cute!

Feeling of the Day: EXCITED AGAIN!

SALMONSDAY (THE BIG DAY!)

Grrr. It took me half an hour to get Finley into
his shark costume. Then as soon as it was
on he did a huge pebbly business in it so I had
to take it off and clean it and put it on again.
Finally we were ready to go.

'Come on, boy,' I said, tugging his lead.

Finley refused to budge. Mum said she
thought he must be teething, he was being so
crotchety. So I had to carry him all the way
across Ripple Reef to Herring Hall, where Pets
Factor was being held. We got there just as the

Pet Fancy Dress was starting, and I managed to drag a very grumpy Finley on stage. All the other pets were standing in a row, being well behaved. We were next to Angie Angelfish. Angie's sea snail, Aurora, looked very posh in a seaweed tutu and shell tiara.

'What do we have to do?' I whispered to Angie, who was nervously eyeing Finley in his shark costume.

'When the music starts, you have to swim up and down at the front of the stage so the audience can see the costume,' she whispered, edging away so that Aurora was in between her and Finley. I remembered she wasn't all that keen on sharks.

'He's not a real shark,' I began to tell her, but at that moment Bob Monkfish, the Pets Factor host, swished on to the stage, bowing

and smiling. Everyone clapped, because he is a VIF – Very Important Fish. He is the mayor of Ripple Reef.

'Let's get down to business!' Bob Monkfish cried. I looked at him in horror. Was he going to do a poo on the stage or something?! But he just looked at his clipboard.

'Up first we have a late entry . . . Darcy Dolphin and Finley!'

'Come on, Fin . . .' I tugged Finley's lead.

Then the most awful thing happened.

Finley, who had been watching Aurora out of the corner of his eye, suddenly pounced forward and snatched her up in his mouth!

Angie screamed. The audience screamed. Bob Monkfish screamed.

Finley shot off towards the front of the

stage with Aurora in his mouth, yanking me after him. He was about to whizz out over the heads of the crowd, when everything suddenly went dark.

'**DROP THE SNAIL!**' a deep voice boomed above my head. Finley froze, a guilty look on his face.

I looked up. Flippering fishsticks! The biggest, toothiest, terrifying-est shark I had ever seen was swimming right over me!

As you can imagine, there was **Total Panic**. Squids squirted ink. Sea cucumbers squirted goo. Cuttlefish changed colour.

The huge shark waggled a fin sternly. 'OPEN...'

Finley opened his mouth.

For a moment nothing happened. Then a rather dented tiara appeared, followed by the rest of Aurora. She crawled out of Finley's mouth and slithered into a corner, where she began eating her tutu. I don't know if that's normal behaviour for snails but she didn't look hurt, anyway.

'Hurrah!!' Everyone cheered, except Angie, who fainted.

So it turns out that Finley is not a dogfish

after all. He's a shark! And his name is actually Fang. The big shark was his mum, and of course I then had to explain to her about finding Finley in the Kelp Forest. I was a bit scared about doing that. I thought she might be really cross and eat me or something. But she didn't.

'I'm just soooo happy to have my little Fangy-wangy back safe again,' she said, giving him a cuddle that would have crushed a smaller fish.

I feel sort of sad about it all – although of course it's good he's back with his family.

Sigh. And I'm back to the lonely life again.

Feeling of the Day: SAD AND LONELY. ☹

SPONGEDAY

Started the day still feeling **sad** and **lonely**.
Finley's food bowl and lead were by my bed,
which made me feel **sadder** and **lonelier**
than ever.

Dad kept saying, 'Plenty more fish in the
sea, Darcy.' I think he thought he was being
helpful but he wasn't. Mum was nice, though.
She let me watch my favourite film, *Diary of a
Shrimpy Squid*, three times before lunch! Then
there was a knock on the door.

Mum opened it. It was Finley's – sorry,

Fang's – mum! She had Fang with her and was carrying a big box. I hid behind Mum because I thought maybe Fang's mum had changed her mind and decided to eat me after all.

My mum started apologising straight away.

'Mrs Shark, I'm sorry Darcy took Finley – I mean Fang . . .'

Mrs Shark smiled. 'It's okay, Mrs Dolphin. I know she didn't mean any harm. And she was very kind to Fang – even though he can be . . . difficult.'

Fang flashed me a sharky grin. (Why did I ever think he was a dogfish?!)

Mrs Shark peered round Mum. 'Darcy?'

I came out.

'I saw how upset you were to lose Fang,' she went on. 'So I've brought you something.'

She handed me the box. I took it, then nearly dropped it.

'It moved!' I yelped.

'Open it,' she said, smiling.

Nervously, I lifted the lid. Inside was a funny little fish that looked a bit like a shark with a flat head. He blew me a friendly bubble.

'Meet Remy the remora,' Mrs Shark said. 'Remoras make great pets for sharks and dolphins. He'll get very attached to you!'

As if to demonstrate, Remy darted out of the box and stuck himself to my side.

I turned to Mum. 'Aw, can I keep him? Please? Please? Please? Please? Please? Pl-'

'Stop, Darcy!' Mum put her fin to her forehead. 'I don't know . . . pets are such trouble . . .'

'Oh, he won't be any trouble,' Mrs Shark said. 'He'll be useful! His favourite game is cleaning up.'

Mum's face lit up. 'Really?! Well, in that case . . .'

PHEE-WEE PHEE-WEE PHWEEEEEE!

I squeaked, which roughly translated means: 'YOU ARE THE BEST MUM EVER!!!!'

So I finally have a pet. Remy and I will be friends for EVER – I just know it! He really is my Perfect Pet.

Feeling of the Day: FINTASTIC!

WEEK 2:
My Dream Role

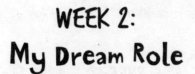

MONKFISHDAY

PHEE-WEEEEE! Happy

Monkfishday, everyone! Today is my first

proper day of being a pet owner. I think Remy

was just as excited about this as I was. From

the moment I woke up he attached himself to

my side and refused to let go – Mum had to

tempt him off with a bowl of Swimalot pet food

so I could go to school. I only just made it in

time for the bell!

After she took the register, Miss Carp

gathered us round.

'Now, everyone,' she said. 'I hope you remember that this Spongeday we are doing a special performance of the school play in the Ripple Reef Theatre. That gives us seven days to prepare. The auditions are in two days' time, on Whalesday, so you will need to have learned your lines by then.'

Flippering fishsticks! The school play – how did I miss that?

'What's the play?' I whispered to Myrtle Turtle, who sits next to me. She poked her head out of her shell and rolled her eyes.

'Finderella!'

I gasped. 'I've *always* wanted to play Finderella . . .'

Miss Carp said loudly that if certain small fry did not stop whispering they would be on

49

Whale Cleaning Duty, so we stopped.

Walter the School Whale brings children who live off the reef into school. He's always covered in barnacles and cleaning him is one of the worst jobs in the world. I know this because I have been on Whale Cleaning Duty a LOT.

Miss Carp continued. 'Remember, the list of parts is on the library door and it's already looking quite full. Anyone who wants to audition and hasn't put their name down must do so before the end of the day,' she said just as the bell rang for lunch.

I zoomed out of that classroom and over to the library faster than a wahoo*! The list was there.

* Wahoo: The wahoo is a super-cool racing fish! It's the third fastest fish in the sea. It has a pointy nose and silver go-faster stripes. Dad says he used to be able to beat wahoos in races but Mum says that is a Big Fat Fib.

AUDITION LIST

Scary Sisters – Bonnie Blobfish, Harriet Hagfish

Fairy Codmother – Myrtle Turtle

Prince Herring – ....

Finderella – Bertha Bream, Clara Cod, Angie Angelfish, Molly Mackerel, Polly Parrotfish, Delia Damselfish, Rhonda Redfin, Lottie Lobster, blah blah blah etc . . .

Well, you get the picture – almost every girl in school wanted to play Finderella! And no one wanted to be Prince Herring. I put my name down for Finderella too. Then I had a **brainwave** and put Ozzie's name down for Prince Herring. He'd make a good prince!

While I was there I got a copy of *Finderella* from the library. Miss Angler, the librarian, glared at me.

'I need it back on Turtlesday, *without fail*,' she said in her dangerous voice.

'Yes, miss,' I said. No one wants to be in Miss Angler's bad books. She has teeth twice as long and three times as sharp as a shark's.

I took the book home but Diddy was watching the new Starfish Wars on telly and I totally love that film! So I didn't get round to learning my lines. Oh well – I've got all day tomorrow!

Feeling of the Day: THEATRICAL.

TUNASDAY

At break time today I tried to learn my lines but Angie Angelfish kept distracting me by flouncing about, saying things like, 'Fair Prince, 'tis midnight and I must away . . .'

That doesn't even make sense! Angie has obviously not read the script properly. The role is mine, I just know it.

After break, Miss Carp read out the list of names for the audition.

When she read out Ozzie's name, all the boys laughed. Ozzie went all multi-coloured.

He does that when he's stressed. Maybe I shouldn't have put his name down. But he WILL make a great prince!

I went home, vowing to learn my lines tonight. But just as I was about to start practising, there was a knock on the door.

It was Ozzie. (He was still a bit of an odd colour.)

'Myrtle told me you put my name down to play Prince Herring!' he moaned. 'I don't want to! I'm useless at acting.'

'No you're not,' I said, feeling slightly guilty. 'You'll make a great prince.'

'Everyone's laughing at me.'

'No they're not. They're . . . happy for you, that's all.'

Ozzie didn't look convinced. Anyway, Mum

asked him to stay to tea and then he wanted to watch Starfish Wars, so of course I had to as well. Which meant I still didn't get to learn my lines! I will just have to stay awake really late tonight and learn them.

Feeling of the day: YAWN . . .

WHALESDAY

Double disaster this morning!

One: I fell asleep, so did not learn my lines last night.

Two: Remy has munched massive chunks out of the Finderella book. Miss Angler is LITERALLY going to eat me alive.

I read what was left of the play in between mouthfuls of prawnflakes. I will just have to make up the rest. That's what proper actors do. They call it improvising. And I'll have to fix the book up somehow before Turtlesday – well,

I'll worry about that later.

Swam to school with Myrtle. When we got there, Miss Cuttle, the drama teacher, told everyone who was auditioning for the roles of Finderella and the Fairy Codmother to go to the hall. Myrtle seemed quite nervous, even though she has learned all her lines and is the only one auditioning for the Fairy Codmother anyway, so she's bound to get it.

I was first up! We swam on to the stage.

'When you're ready, girls,' Miss Cuttle called.

Myrtle: Finderella SHALL go to the ball, and be the best-dressed fish of all. *(waves invisible wand)*

Me: I hope the Prince isn't too boring, or I'll be in a corner snoring. *(yawns)*

Myrtle: (whispering) Finderella doesn't say

that! You're supposed to say you like the outfit.

Me: Okay, okay. Um ... my golden flippers

are so swish! I'll be a really stylish fish.

Miss Cuttle: Darcy, Darcy, that's not right.

Didn't you learn your lines last night?

Everyone: Awkward silence.

Me: I may not have learned a single line,

but I think you'll agree I'm doing just fine!

Miss Cuttle: NEXT PLEASE!

61

I'm not sure Myrtle and Miss Cuttle understand improvisation. But I thought it went quite well, all in all. We find out tomorrow morning who got the part.

Aargh, I can't wait that long!

This evening I had to try and mend the Finderella book, and write in all the bits that Remy had eaten. Aunt Ditzy came round and helped me with the writing. It still looks a bit chewed, but it's quite dark in the library so hopefully Miss Angler won't notice. I don't fancy being eaten alive.

Feeling of the Day: HOPEFUL.

TURTLESDAY

This morning I got to school early so I could sneak into the library and put the Finderella book back before Miss Angler arrived. I raced to the classroom just in time for register, and then Miss Carp read out the audition results.

'Fairy Codmother – Myrtle Turtle.'

Everyone clapped.

'Prince Herring – Ozzie Octopus!'

Ozzie turned bright orange, green and purple.

'And Finderella will be . . .'

Please, please, please! Me me me! I held my breath.

'Angie Angelfish.'

I was hit by a tidal wave of misery. Of all the fish in the sea, why did it have to be Angie who got to play Finderella?!

But it got worse.

'Darcy, I have decided that you will play the coach.'

The COACH?! **Flippering fishsticks**,

I don't want to be a boring old coach. The coach doesn't have any lines to say, it just has to take Finderella to the ball and park itself outside while Finderella has all the fun.

At breaktime Angie Angelfish swished about like a princess, followed by a huge shoal of silly sardines asking for her autograph.

Hmmf. No one wants *my* autograph.

Ozzie was grumpy too. He said his lines are slushy.

'Listen to this: "Oh Finders, you're my fishy queen, with your shell-like ears and scales seaweed green." How soppy is that?'

'At least you have lines,' I said. 'All I have to do is park. Even plankton can park!'

We had our first rehearsal after school.

It wasn't a huge success. Angie's sardine fan club turned up and squealed madly whenever she came on stage, which meant she kept forgetting her lines. Prince Herring's tentacles got tangled up. Bonnie Blobfish and Harriet Hagfish, the Scary Sisters, got into an argument about who was scariest. The Fairy Codmother went into her shell and wouldn't come out.

I didn't do too badly. Angie only fell off my back three times. Parking is a bit harder than I thought.

By the end of the rehearsal, Miss Cuttle was bright purple, yellow, blue and pink,

and quivering under a rock. Like Ozzie, she

changes colour when she's stressed.

I know how she feels. I may do the same.

Feeling of the day: GRUMPY.

FLOUNDERSDAY

I lay awake last night for aaaages thinking
about the whole Finderella thing, and Mum
had to come and turn off the lanternfish. But I
came to an Important Decision. I am not going
to whinge and moan any more. I'm going to be
the Best Coach Ever. So I got up early and
practised my parking moves. As usual, Remy
had attached himself to my side.

'Forward, reverse, forward, reverse . . .
brake! Reverse, turn, forward, reverse . . .
whoops, sorry Remy!'

I'd squished Remy. He unattached himself

from me and shot crossly off into the toy cave.

I needed more parking practice, so after I'd

stuffed Remy full of prawnflakes till he wasn't

cross any more, I gave Ozzie and Myrtle a lift

to school. I parked pretty perfectly outside the

gate, though I say so myself. Miss Carp was watching.

'If there's one thing to be said for you, Darcy, it's that you have a Positive Mental Attitude,' she said. I don't exactly know what that is, but it sounds good!

At lunchtime I offered rides to everyone in the playground so I could practise some more coach moves. It was fun. I think I might start my own taxi service!

As I swam back to class after lunch, I saw a crowd of excited sardines hovering around the art cupboard.

'What's going on?' I pushed the sardines
out of the way and opened the door.

Angie was hiding behind a stack of squid ink
bottles. She looked relieved when she saw me.

'What's wrong?' I asked.

She burst into tears.
'Those sardines won't
leave me alone! And
they're making me
forget my lines!'

Poor Angie. Fame
is obviously getting to
her. Maybe it's not such
a bad thing after all, being
the coach. I opened the door and shooed the
sardines away. Then I had a **brainwave**.
I suggested maybe Angie could come to my

house on the weekend and I'd help her learn her lines.

'I'll get Ozzie and Myrtle to come too, then we can all practise together.'

She looked a bit happier. My Positively Mental Attitude must be rubbing off on her.

This evening Mum said that Angie, Ozzie and Myrtle can come over tomorrow, but to remember that Aunt Ditzy is visiting, and not to drink anything she might bring with her. Last time Dad had one of Aunt Ditzy's herbal juices he was trumping stinkers for days.

Feeling of the day: POSITIVELY MENTAL.

SALMONSDAY

Aunt Ditzy arrived – late, as always. She wafted in, wearing a red seaweed poncho and an enormous sea-anemone-encrusted hat. And she brought some evil-looking seaweed smoothies with her.

'They're good for boosting confidence,' she said, holding one of the foaming green drinks out to me. 'Try one, Darcy.'

'No, thank you,' I said. 'My confidence is fine.'

Angie, Ozzie and Myrtle arrived five

minutes later. Angie had brought a copy of Finderella with her. It had bite marks on the cover and had been stuck together with jellytape.

'Where did you get that book?' I asked.

'I lost my copy, so I borrowed this one from the library,' she said 'Why?'

I hesitated. I knew it was the copy that Remy had chewed up and that Aunt Ditzy and I had rewritten.

Should I tell Angie it was a slightly different version to the one she'd been using? But Aunt Ditzy and I fixed it up pretty well, I thought. I felt quite proud of some of the rewritten bits!

'No reason,' I said. 'Right, let's go. I'll be Scary Sister 1.'

Aunt Ditzy, who had been listening in, said she would be Scary Sister 2.

It started out okay.

Scary Sister 1: Finderella, you're such a bore. Go to the kitchen and scrub the floor.

Finderella: You do it, you lazy thing. Don't disturb me, I'm studying.

Scary Sister 2: It is Prince Herring's ball tonight. I must do my hair. I look a fright!

Finderella: I'm not invited, but I don't care. I've better things to do than style my hair ... hang on, this is all different to the book I had before! Finderella is supposed to be sad that she can't go to the ball!

'We changed it a bit,' I said. 'Aunt Ditzy thought Finderella should be a bit less ... wimpy.'

Angie went pale. 'I think I'm going to faint,' she said weakly.

Aunt Ditzy rushed over to her. 'What you need is a confidence boost,' she said. 'Here, have one of these ...'

'NO – DON'T DRINK IT, ANGIE!!!' I yelled.

But before I could stop her, Aunt Ditzy
had poured a whole seaweed smoothie down
Angie's throat.

Angie immediately went a very funny
purple colour and groaning noises started
coming from her tummy, so that was the end of
rehearsals. Well, I guess we'll just have to see
what happens tomorrow :-/

Feeling of the Day: JELLYFISH TUMMY
WOBBLES . . .

SPONGEDAY

Showtime! I was so excited I couldn't eat my prawnflakes, so Remy ate them instead. I think he prefers them to Swimalot. I swam to school with Ozzie and Myrtle, but when we arrived there was a **commotion** going on. A crowd of pupils were hovering around outside the girls' toilets, whispering nervously.

'What's happening?' I asked Bertha Bream.

'Angie Angelfish went in, and five seconds later there was a loud gurgling noise,' Bertha whispered. 'And now stinky green bubbles are

coming from under the door . . .'

Oh dear. That's why we never drink
Aunt Ditzy's smoothies. Myrtle and I pushed
through the crowd and went in to find Angie in
a corner, bubbles of green gas popping out of
her rear end.

'I'm not going on stage like this!' she
wailed.

'But you're the main character,' Myrtle
said. 'There won't be anyone to play Finderella.'

Angie grabbed me. 'YOU could play
Finderella,' she said.

'I'm the coach,' I said, shaking my head.
'I've been practising really hard to be the Best
Coach Ever!'

'Oh please, Darcy,' Angie begged as another
stream of bubbles erupted from her bottom.

She crossed her fins. 'I'm not going on stage, and that's final.'

'Well ... I guess I'll have to, then ... but if I'm playing Finderella, who will be the coach?' I said.

Myrtle laughed. 'You'll just have to swim to the ball, silly!'

So I got to play Finderella, after all!

Ozzie did make a good Prince – like I said he would. He didn't remember any of his lines, but that was okay, I just talked non-stop so he didn't have to say anything.

There was one scary bit when Miss Angler burst on to the stage waving the tatty-looking copy of Finderella and looking murderous. She chased me round and round, shouting that she

was going to eat me alive, but then everyone

cheered – they thought she was an extra

Scary Sister!

At the end we all lined up and took a bow.

When we came off stage, Miss Angler came

over to me. I was a bit worried that she was

still going to eat me alive. But then to my

surprise, she asked me for my autograph!

She said she changed her mind about eating

me when she realised that actually the play
was much better now I'd rewritten it.

'I always thought Finderella was a bit of a
wet fish,' she said as I signed the half-eaten
copy of Finderella she handed me. 'I much
preferred your version!'

Angie is still producing stinky green
bubbles, but they're getting smaller. Aunt
Ditzy asked her if she felt any more confident,

but Angie gave her a terrified look and shot

under a rock so I guess that answered THAT

question.

Feeling of the Day: HAVING A BALL!

WEEK 3:
The Rumbling Reef
Mystery

R-R-R-R-RUMMMMBLE!

MONKFISHDAY

PHEE-WEEEEE! Me again. Today

has been interesting, because there are

mysterious happenings on the reef – and

no one knows what to make of them!

It all started this morning as we were

having breakfast. Dad was reading the Daily

Echo. Diddy was throwing prawnflakes at

Remy. Remy was chasing his tail, when –

R-R-R-R-RUMMMMMMBLE!

The whole reef shook!

Dad looked up from his newspaper. 'Did

someone say something?'

Then –

R-R-R-R-RUMMMMMBLE!

Remy shot to my side and latched on so hard I yelped.

'Earthquake!' Dad exclaimed. 'Under the table, everyone!'

I was pretty scared – I'd never been in an earthquake before. Was the sea floor going to open up and swallow us?! We all huddled under the table and waited, but nothing happened. After five minutes we swam out and looked around. The sea floor was fine.

'Can't have been an earthquake,' Dad said, looking puzzled. Then he turned to me and said very seriously, 'Maybe Angie Angelfish is still suffering the after-effects of Ditzy's seaweed smoothie.'

So in assembly this morning I kept a sharp eye on Angie, but although she popped out a couple of very small green bubbles, they weren't exactly earth-shaking.

Back in the classroom, everyone was talking about the strange rumbling noise. No one could think what it could be! And then –

R-R-R-R-RUMMMMBLE!

The whole class bolted under the desks and quivered like jellyfish. But the sea floor still didn't open up, so finally Miss Carp said it was safe to come out. Everyone did, except Angie, who said she was going to stay under the desk all day because her mum always says better safe than sorry.

Miss Carp gathered the rest of us round.

'Now, pupils, as some of you may know, this week is Whale Week ...'

I tried to listen but I kept thinking about the rumbling. What in the sea could it be? An underwater volcano?

Miss Carp was still wittering away. 'Whale Week celebrates the Amazing Awesomeness of Whales ...'

Maybe it was the end of the world ...

'DARCY! Are you listening to me?'

I jerked to attention. 'Yes, miss.'

'To mark this event, I want everyone to do a little project on whales. Anything you like. A picture, a poem, a dance . . .'

R-R-R-R-RUMMMMMBLE!

Back under the desks we went. This happened about sixteen times! Angie had the right idea after all.

Feeling of the Day: MYSTIFIED.

TUNASDAY

The rumbling is STILL happening! No one knows what it is, and this evening it's been joined by another noise too.

Sort of like this:

OOOOOOooooooooooooo...

I thought maybe the oooohing noise was Ozzie doing his trumpetfish practice. So I went round to the Lucky Gull (the shipwreck where he lives) to investigate.

Ozzie wasn't playing his trumpetfish. He was writing. He's very quick at it because he

can do eight sentences at a time!

'What are you writing?' I asked.

'A poem about whales. Shall I read it to you?' He cleared his throat.

'*I like whales,*

Especially their tails.

They are quite gigantic.

They live in the Atlantic.

. . . What do you think?'

'Great,' I said. 'I like the rhymes.'

R-R-R-R-RUMMMMMBLE!

ₒₒₒₒOOOOOOOOOOHHHH . . .

I jumped.

'Forget poetry – we've got to find out what those noises are . . .'

I heard a familiar clicking noise. Then,

'Dar-cy! Din-ner!'

'Fishsticks! That's Mum,' I said to Ozzie. 'I have to go.'

Over dinner, Dad showed Mum an article in the Daily Echo.

The headline read: **RUMBLING REEF MYSTERY DEEPENS!**

'I do wish they'd find out what it was,' said Mum. 'Eat your fish fingers, Darcy, they'll make your brain bigger.'

I said my brain was already big and I was going to use it to solve the Rumbling Reef Mystery.

'Good idea,' Dad said. 'But use your big brain to do your homework first.'

Sigh. Do top detectives have to do homework before they solve mysteries? I don't think so! I decided to do a whale picture, but I didn't have any paints so I made a collage out of prawnflakes. Ingenious, I thought! By the time I finished there wasn't a chance to do any detective work, because it was bedtime.

Feeling of the Day: ARTISTIC.

WHALESDAY

This morning I had another puzzle to deal with.
My whale picture had vanished. Remy was
skulking about with a guilty look in his eye and a
prawnflake on his nose. Then he barfed a load
of half-digested prawnflakes on the floor.

So that was *that* mystery solved.

Miss Carp will not be happy.

At school, the rumbling and oohing noises

were even louder than yesterday. Ozzie

practically had to shout his poem to the class.

'I LIKE . . .

R-R-R-RUMMMBLE

. . . WHALES, ESPECIALLY . . .

OOOOOOHHHHHHH . . .

. . . THEIR TAILS . . .'

'Thank you, Ozzie,' said Miss Carp when

he'd finished. 'Who's next . . . Darcy?'

So I had to tell Miss Carp that Remy ate

my homework. I even showed her some of the

half-digested prawnflakes.

She said it sounded like a fishy story. I said

it was more of a *prawny* story.

Then she put me on Whale Cleaning Duty at

lunchtime for being cheeky, and for not doing

my homework.

Eurrrgh. As I think I've mentioned before, Whale Cleaning Duty means scraping barnacles off Walter the School Whale. The barnacles stick like glue *and* they call you rude names. It's the worst job in the ocean! The only good thing about it is that I can have a proper moan to Walter about stuff. He's an excellent listener.

After I'd eaten my lunch, I grumpily swam round the back of school and over the edge of the reef to where Walter lives. I could see his huge shape just ahead, near the surface. Suddenly there was yet another rumble!

As I swam closer to Walter the rumbling noise got louder . . . and louder . . . and then I realised – the rumbling was coming *from* Walter! And as he loomed into view I saw that instead of his usual deep blue colour, he was a

sickly green.

He turned a sad face to me and said,

'ₒₒₒₒₒₒOOOOOOOOOOOOHHHH ...!

My tummy ...'

Another loud rumble made my teeth rattle.

'It won't stop rumbling,' Walter groaned. 'I

can hardly move and I haven't eaten so much

as a prawn in days ...'

Poor Walter. Whale-sized tummy ache

can't be fun! Then I had a **brainwave**.

'I'll be your doctor,' I exclaimed. 'I can bring

you medicine and do . . . um . . . other medical
stuff.'

Another reef-shaking rumble rippled
through Walter. He moaned. 'Maybe you should
get a *real* doctor, Darcy,' he began.

I patted one of his fins.

'Don't worry,' I said. 'I know what I'm doing.
I'll look it up in a book tomorrow at school. You'll
be as fit as a fiddler crab in no time!'

Walter didn't look exactly happy, but then
I suppose he is ill, poor thing. I'm quite excited
about being a whale doctor, though!

Feeling of the Day: CARING.

TURTLESDAY

Woohoo, I solved the **Mystery of the Rumbling Reef**. Just call me Detective Darcy!

Actually, call me Doctor Darcy – because now I have the extremely important job of making Walter well again.

I told Mum and Dad about Walter last night. They were pleased to find out that the sea bed wasn't about to swallow us up after all. Then this morning Mum said she was going to phone Doctor Dab. I told her not to because I was going to cure Walter myself.

'Darcy, don't be silly. You don't know a thing about sick whales,' said Mum. 'Now off you go to school.'

'I'll find a book about it,' I said as I went out, but Mum didn't listen. She was on the phone to the doctor. Honestly, she is so NEGATIVE sometimes! I think she needs a dose of my Positive Mental Attitude.

At morning break I went to the school library and asked Miss Angler if she had any books on whale diseases. She gave me a funny look and said no, but she did have one called *How to Train Your Goldfish*. I looked at the contents. Aha. Page 12 – Goldfish Diseases.

I turned to the page and read, 'Is your goldfish upside-down? You may be over-feeding it.'

Hmm.

Nothing about

whales with rumbling tummies, though.

After school I took the goldfish book with me when I went to see Walter. Doctor Dab was there already with Miss Carp and Mr Snapper, the head teacher. They were all scratching their heads and ummming and ahhing.

I showed Doctor Dab the book and asked if he had checked whether Walter was upside-down or not. He said that whales were a different kettle of fish to goldfish, because in fact they weren't fish at all, they were mammals – just like us dolphins. I sneaked a quick glance at Walter anyway but he looked like he was the right way up.

'Say "Aaah",' said Doctor Dab to Walter. Walter opened his mouth.

'AAAAHHHHHHHH!'

Doctor Dab swam into Walter's cave-like mouth and disappeared. A minute later, Walter did a reef-rumbling burp, and the doctor rocketed back out at top speed.

'It's trapped wind. He needs medicine,' he said, picking himself up and throwing Walter a nervous glance.

'What sort of medicine?' I asked. But Miss Carp told me rather sharply to leave the doctor alone and go and play.

Tsk. Grown-ups are so annoying sometimes. I will read up about medicine for trapped wind the minute I get into school tomorrow morning.

Feeling of the Day:

MEDICINAL.

FLOUNDERSDAY

In the morning, the rumbling was worse than
ever! Poor Walter must be feeling terrible,
I thought. I swam to school really fast, and
when I got there Miss Carp let me go on the
aquanet to look up whale tummy medicine. I got
665,000 results. But I didn't have time to read
them all because Miss Carp said we had to go
to the hall, as a visitor was coming to talk to us.

When we got there, Miss Carp clapped her
fins.

'Quiet please, everyone! We have a

celebrity chef in school today. She is going
to show you how to make a recipe from her
book ...'

A dolphin dressed in a seaweed poncho and
sea-anemone-encrusted hat swam on stage.

'Greetings, everyone!' she called. 'Now I'm
going to show you how to whip up a tasty and
nutritious **Super Seaweed Smoothie**!'

I gaped. I saw Ozzie and Myrtle gaping too.

'Isn't that your aunt Ditzy?' whispered Myrtle. In the row behind me I heard Angie whimper in fright.

Myrtle whispered, 'Doesn't Miss Carp know what Aunt Ditzy's smoothie did to Angie last week?'

I shook my head. 'Obviously not!'

Everyone shuffled nervously as Aunt Ditzy threw a bucket-load of seaweed into a giant clam shell, along with some other ingredients.

'. . . a squirt of hagfish slime . . . pickled jellyfish stings . . . seven pints of curried mud . . .'

A stinky, brownish-green sludge began oozing over the top of the shell.

'Hey presto! One whale-sized Super

Seaweed Smoothie,' she pronounced. 'Who'd
like to try some? I made enough for everyone!'

Silence.

'Come along, be brave, pupils,' Miss Carp
called.

More silence.

'Right, I'll pick someone ...'

There was a thud behind me. Angie had
fainted.

Aunt Ditzy looked glum. I felt sorry for her, but really, who'd want to drink something that made bright green bubbles explode out of your bottom?

And then, DING! I had a WHALE-SIZED **brainwave**!

I put my fin up.

'Aunt Ditzy, can I take the smoothie home with me?'

'Are you mad?' Ozzie whispered. 'You know what those smoothies do!'

'It's not for me . . . I'll explain later,' I whispered back.

I told Aunt Ditzy that I was taking the Super Seaweed Smoothie home for the family to try. She was delighted. After school I told Ozzie and Myrtle my brainwave.

'Walter's got trapped wind! Aunt Ditzy's Super Seaweed Smoothie might be just the medicine he needs to make him blast it all out!'

Ozzie looked worried and turned a sort of greeny-yellow. 'Or it could make him explode.'

I shook my head. 'Let's go over there now,' I said. But when we got out of school, Mum was waiting at the gates with a sulky-looking Remy in tow. I'd completely forgotten it was his check-up at the vets.

'We'll have to go tomorrow,' I said to Ozzie and Myrtle.

Feeling of the Day: OPTIMISTIC.

SALMONSDAY

This morning I told Mum and Dad my plans for making Walter well again. I showed them the clam shell full of Super Seaweed Smoothie.

Dad asked if I was trying to kill Walter off. 'It looks even more poisonous than usual.'

'Medicine isn't supposed to look nice,' I pointed out.

'It's not supposed to escape, though, is it?' Mum said, pointing at the shell. Large globs of brownish green sludge seemed to be trying to crawl over the side.

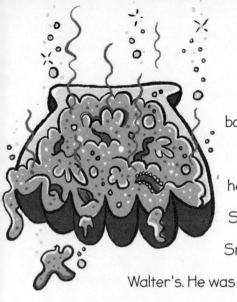

I shoved them back in quickly.

Ozzie and Myrtle helped me carry the Super Seaweed Smoothie over to Walter's. He was right where I'd left him, and the rumbling coming from his huge tummy was deafening.

'Walter, we've brought you some medicine,' I yelled over the rumbling.

We tipped the seaweed smoothie into Walter's mouth.

'OOOOOOH!' he moaned.

We waited expectantly. The rumbling started to get louder . . . and louder . . . and **louder** . . .

'SWIM AWAY!' I yelled. 'HE'S GOING TO BLOW!!!'

BOOOOOOOOOOM!!!!

As we swam away to a safe distance, a blast of water knocked me sideways. I turned round to see the biggest green bubble EVER pop out of Walter's rear end!

Then there was silence.

'Is he okay?' whispered Myrtle. We stayed put for a couple of minutes, but nothing happened, so we swam slowly back towards Walter. He had a very surprised look on his face and a little stream of green bubbles coming from his bottom.

'Walter? Are you okay?' I said.

Walter's huge eye turned towards me.

Then he smiled a big whaley smile.

'Do you know, I really think I am,' he said.

Feeling of the Day: HAVING A WHALE
OF A TIME!

SPONGEDAY

I had just finished breakfast this morning when there was a knock on the door. It was Ozzie and Myrtle. Ozzie was holding a copy of the Daily Echo.

'Darcy – you and Aunt Ditzy have made the papers!' he cried.

We all rushed over to look at the newspaper.

'SEAWEED SMOOTHIE SAVES WHALE,' it said in big letters on the front page. There was a picture of Walter, grinning his huge whaley grin!

Dad read the article aloud:

'Darcy Dolphin and her aunt, Ditzy Dolphin, make a super smooth double act, according to Walter the School Whale. Walter's tummy rumbles have been heard all over the reef for days, but one dose of Ditzy's Super Seaweed Smoothie and the whale was back to his normal happy, healthy self in no time.

'"It was Darcy's idea to give me the smoothie," Walter told our reporter. "I had a bad case of trapped wind, but one of Ditzy's smoothies cleared it out. They're both heroes!"'

Mum hugged me. 'Well done, you clever thing.'

'Good for you, Darcy,' Dad said. 'Who would have thought that Aunt Ditzy's Stinky – sorry,

Super Seaweed Smoothies could cure a whale's tummy ache!'

There was another knock on the door. Aunt Ditzy burst in, looking slightly dazed. **'PHEE-WEEEEE!** Do you have any idea what's happening?!' she exclaimed. 'There's a crowd of whales outside my house wanting to buy my book!'

We rushed to the window. A humongously long line of whales was queuing all down Ripple Reef Road. I grinned.

'You'd better start writing some more recipes, Aunt Ditzy,' I said. 'You're famous.'

I showed her the newspaper. Her eyes nearly popped out. Then she smiled happily.

'I'd better go and sort out these whales, then, hadn't I! Oh – and you're all invited for a celebration lunch . . .'

She darted out of the door.

'What *is* for lunch, Ditzy?' Mum called after her.

'Super Seaweed Smoothies,' I heard her shout as she disappeared between the whales.

Remy and I are now officially in hiding, in Diddy's toy cave. At least until after lunch.

Wow, I just read through my diary and I can't believe how much has happened!

1. I got a new, perfect pet . . .

2. I got to play Finderella . . .

3. I saved Walter . . .

4. Best of all, Aunt Ditzy's recipe book is a

whale of a success!

'And all that in only three weeks,' I said to

Remy, who was curled up next to me. He just

sort of snuffled happily and gave me a lick.

Next week I'm going to do even more exciting

stuff and write it all down, every single second!

I wonder what adventures we'll have, Remy?

Remy ... what are you doing? Oh no, Remy –

please don't eat my fintastic diary!

Feeling of the D

DIVE INTO DARCY'S UNDERWATER WORLD!

MEET THE CHARACTERS

Name: Darcy Dolphin

Likes: Helping, talking, acting, wave-jumping, playing with my friends, playing with Remy, writing my Fintastic Diary!

Dislikes: Super Seaweed Smoothies, Whale Cleaning Duty, barnacles

Favourite food: Jiggling Jellies

Favourite film: Diary of a Shrimpy Squid

Pet: Remy (remora fish)

Name: Ozzie Octopus

Likes: Working out hard sums, writing poems, playing trumpetfish

Dislikes: Acting, shopping, sardines

Favourite food: Fish fingers

Favourite film: Starfish Wars

Pet: Cuke
(sea cucumber)

Name: Myrtle Turtle

Likes: Reading, dressing up, playing Hide 'n' Squeak

Dislikes: Arguments, bogies, sneezing

Favourite food: Prawnflakes

Favourite film: Teenage Mutant Ninja Turtles

Pet: Squishy (vampire squid)

HOW TO DRAW A DOLPHIN

Start with big, bright eyes.
Did you know that dolphins' eyes can move independently of each other?

Now add a nose.
Bottlenose dolphins like Darcy have a long nose called a 'beak'. (Useful for poking your nose into things and talking!).

Don't forget to leave a gap in the body for the fin!
A dolphin's large forehead is called a 'melon'.

All dolphins have tails.
Darcy uses her tail like a big flipper to propel her through the water (and often into trouble . . .).

4.

5. **Time for the fin!**
The dorsal fin helps keep dolphins swimming upright.

6.

And the pectoral fins help dolphins to turn.
Very useful for playing the coach in Finderella!

Have fun colouring in!
Bottlenose dolphins
are grey with lighter-
coloured bellies. Unlike
Ozzie they don't change
colour when they are
scared!

7.

8.

**Use your imagination to add extra
details to your dolphin character.**
Darcy has freckles, a schoolbag and
fintastic diary!

ABOUT THE AUTHOR

Name: Sam Watkins

Likes: Writing stories, snails, snorkelling, chocolate biscuits, lizards, dangling off cliffs on ropes and weird-shaped vegetables

Dislikes: Sprouts, winter, herbal tea, cling film, and zombies

Favourite sea creature: Apart from dolphins, I totally LOVE octopuses. They are extremely intelligent and can squeeze themselves through the tiniest of tiny cracks. They have even been known to escape from their tanks in aquariums!

ABOUT THE ILLUSTRATOR

Name: Vicky Barker

Likes: Drawing and doodling, Marcy (my dog), in fact - all dogs, reading, biscuits, listening to music (and singing really loud in my studio)

Dislikes: Spiders, tomatoes (bleurrrrghhhh), feet, cold weather, and empty biscuit tins

Favourite sea creature: That's too hard! My favourite birthday was spent watching a blue whale, though. That was pretty special.

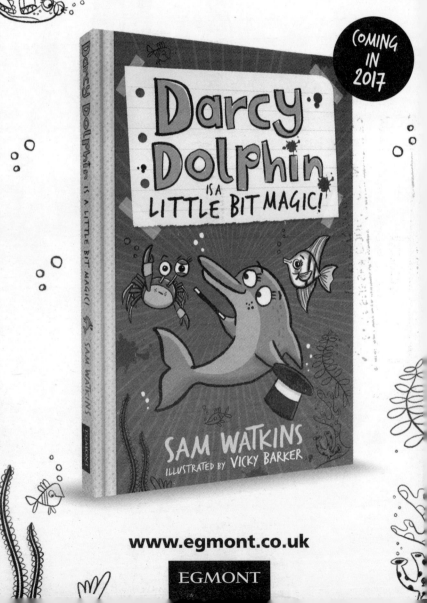